Alice in Wonderland

Retold by Lorraine Horsley

Illustrated by Barbara Bongini

One hot day, Alice wanted
to play with her sister.

"It's too hot," said her sister.

Alice began to feel very,
very sleepy.

Suddenly, a white rabbit ran by.

"Oh, no!" said the White Rabbit. "I'm late!" Then he disappeared down a rabbit hole.

Alice jumped down the hole after him. She could feel herself falling down, down, down. At last she came to a stop.

"That was very odd," she said.

Alice could see doors all around her, but they were locked. She saw a table with a key on it.

Then Alice saw a little door. The key fitted the door, but Alice was too big to go through it.

Alice looked at the table again. This time there was a bottle on it that said DRINK ME.

Alice took a drink.

"Oh my!" she said. "I feel very strange!" Alice was getting smaller and smaller.

13

Soon Alice was so small she could fit through the little door. But she had left the key on the table.

Then Alice saw a little cake with EAT ME on it. She ate it and this time Alice got bigger and bigger.

Alice could now get the key
from the table, but she was
too big to fit through the door.
Suddenly, the White Rabbit
came along.

"Can you help me?" Alice asked,
but when he saw her he ran off.
"I do feel very odd," she said.

17

Alice was getting smaller and
smaller again. She began to cry
and soon she was up to her head
in tears!

Then, Alice saw some animals.

"How very odd!" she said, as she
got out of the tears.

Alice looked up and saw a caterpillar on a mushroom.

She asked the caterpillar if he could make her big again.

"One side will make you bigger," said the caterpillar, "and the other side will make you smaller."

"One side of what?" asked Alice.

"The mushroom," said the caterpillar, and off he went.

Alice ate some of the mushroom. Then she took some more of the mushroom and went on her way.

23

Next, Alice saw a house.
She went inside.

In the house was a duchess
with a baby and a cat.

The cat smiled at Alice.

Suddenly, the Duchess jumped up. "Here!" she said to Alice. "You have the baby. I'm off to play croquet with the Queen!"

Alice looked at the baby. But it wasn't a baby now, it was a pig. It jumped down and ran away.

Alice found the cat up a tree.

"Are you going to play croquet with the Queen?" he asked Alice.

"I don't know," she said.

"I am," smiled the cat. He disappeared but left his smile behind. It was very strange.

Next, Alice found a Mad Hatter and his friends. They were drinking tea and eating cake.

Alice had some tea with them.

Then Alice saw a tree with a door in it. When she went through it she was back by the table with the key to the little door.

"This time I know what to do," said Alice. She began to eat some of the mushroom and got smaller and smaller. At last she could fit through the little door.

35

On the other side of the door were some playing cards. They were painting some white roses red.

"Why are you painting the roses red?" asked Alice.

"The Queen of Hearts wants all roses to be red," they said.

Just then, the Queen of Hearts came by with the Duchess and the White Rabbit.

The Queen looked at the white roses and then at the playing cards. "Off with their heads," she ordered. "And then it is time to play croquet!"

It was a very odd game of croquet. When it was over, only the Queen and Alice were left.

"Now for the trial," said the Queen.

41

On trial was the Knave of Hearts. The Queen said he had stolen her tarts. "Off with his head!" she ordered.

"You can't do that!" said Alice.

"I can!" said the Queen, "and off with your head, too!"

"No!" said Alice. "No, no, NO!"

"Wake up! Wake up, Alice!"

Suddenly, Alice found herself back with her sister.

"Oh, my!" she said, "I have just had the strangest dream..."

How much do you remember about the story of Alice in Wonderland? Answer these questions and find out!

- Who does Alice follow down the rabbit hole?

- What does it say on the bottle that Alice finds?

- Who is sitting on a mushroom?

- What does the Duchess' baby turn into?

- Who is having a tea party?

- Who does Alice play croquet with?

Unjumble these words to make words from the story, then match them to the correct pictures.

Mda Hatret   Wetih Rtbiab   tac

Qunee   Aecil   Deshucs

Read it yourself with Ladybird

Tick the books you've read!

For more confident readers who can read simple stories with help.

Level 3

- YOU won't like this present as much as I DO!
- The Elves and the Shoemaker
- Hansel and Gretel
- Harry and the Bucketful of Dinosaurs
- Jack and the Beanstalk
- The Red Knight
- Furi on Music Island
- Poppet Stows Away
- Rapunzel
- Aladdin
- The Jungle Book
- Roxy and the Great Escape
- Angry Birds: Meet the Chuck!
- Angry Birds: Bomb's Best Birthday

Longer stories for more independent, fluent readers.

Level 4

- I am Inventing an Invention
- Harry and the Dinosaurs United
- Heidi
- Katsuma and the Art Thief
- Luvli and the Glump-a-tron
- The Pied Piper of Hamelin
- Sam and the Robots
- Snow White and the Seven Dwarfs
- The Wizard of Oz
- The Little Mermaid
- Alice in Wonderland
- Oddie The Hero
- Angry Birds: Red and the Great Flung Off
- Angry Birds: Stella

Available on the App Store

The Read it yourself with Ladybird app is now available

ANDROID APP ON Google play

App also available on Android™ devices

Level 4 is ideal for children who are ready to read longer stories with a wider vocabulary and are eager to start reading independently.

Special features:

Full, exciting story

Clear type

Richer, more varied vocabulary

Suddenly, the Duchess jumped up. "Here!" she said to Alice. "You have the baby. I'm off to play croquet with the Queen!"

Alice looked at the baby. But it wasn't a baby now, it was a pig. It jumped down and ran away.

26

27

Longer sentences

"Oh, no!" said the White Rabbit. "I'm late!" Then he disappeared down a rabbit hole.

Alice jumped down the hole after him. She could feel herself falling down, down, down. At last she came to a stop.

"That was very odd," she said.

Detailed illustrations capture the imagination

Educational Consultant: Geraldine Taylor
Book Banding Consultant: Kate Ruttle

A catalogue record for this book is available from the British Library

Published by Ladybird Books Ltd
80 Strand, London, WC2R 0RL
A Penguin Company

001

ISBN: 978-0-72328-800-8

Printed in China